FIREMAN SAM

D0347661

Wheel of Fire

EGMONT

We bring stories to life

First published in Great Britain 2013
This edition published 2015 by Egmont UK Limited,
The Yellow Building, 1 Nicholas Road,
London W11 4AN

ISBN 978 0 6035 7142 8
62096/1
Printed in China

At the Railway Station, Fireman Sam and Penny had just finished polishing Bessie under Officer Steele's eagle eye. Bessie was the oldest fire engine in Pontypandy.

Penny and Sam pushed the old engine along the rails, back into her shed.

"We need to keep you inside, Bessie," Fireman Sam told her. "There is going to be a firework display here tonight!"

Meanwhile, Gareth was
chatting to Charlie and Bronwyn at the café.

"I've been asked to organise the Pontypandy
firework display," said Gareth.

"**Really?**" said Bronwyn, sounding worried.
Her father always set things on fire on Bonfire
Night. "Will you help him?" she whispered quietly
to Charlie.

A little later, Fireman Sam was teaching the children about the Firework Safety Code down at the Fire Station. He showed them a picture of a Catherine wheel.

"What's wrong here?" he asked.

"It's not nailed on properly," replied James.

"Top marks," smiled Sam.

Over at the Railway Station, Gareth didn't know the Firework Safety Code quite as well as James.

"Shouldn't those rockets be further apart?" Charlie asked, as he watched Gareth set up the display.

"No, they're fine," replied Gareth. "I know what I'm doing."

But when Gareth wasn't looking, Charlie moved them further away from each other!

Back at the Fire Station, Fireman Sam had finished his safety talk. He handed out copies of a firework safety leaflet to all the children.

"Read it carefully and have a **safe** night!" he told them.

Meanwhile, Gareth was still busy setting up the fireworks.

"**Aha!** The perfect place," he cried, fixing a Catherine wheel to the door of Bessie's shed. "It's nearly time for the big display!"

"That's what I'm afraid of ..." muttered Charlie, looking worried.

Soon the crowds began to gather at the Railway Station to watch the display.

James checked his leaflet.

"Are you using a safety taper, Grandad?" he asked.

"Of course," nodded Gareth.

WHOOSH! A shower of sparks lit up the sky. The big display had begun ...

Next, Gareth went to light the Catherine wheel.

"**Wait!**" cried James. "It isn't fixed properly!"

"It certainly is!" replied his grandad.

But when Gareth lit the firework,
disaster struck!

It was fixed too tightly
and wouldn't spin
around. Sparks began
to burn Bessie's
shed door ...

Moments later, an emergency call came in at the Fire Station.

"Bessie's shed is on fire!" cried Officer Steele in horror. Fireman Sam, Penny and Officer Steele grabbed their helmets and jumped into Jupiter. There wasn't a second to lose!

As Jupiter screeched up to the Railway Station, Fireman Sam leapt out of the door. He unravelled the hose and took aim.

"Turn it on, Penny!" he ordered.

SWOOSH! A blast of water hit the shed door and the flames began to die down.

Bessie was saved!

"I'm sorry I didn't listen to you about the Catherine wheel," Gareth told James later.

"That's okay, Grandad," grinned James. "Maybe next year I can help you set things up **properly!**"

The End